I can't find it!

Kitty was always losing things. It wasn't that she was careless. Of course not. What happened was this. Things she put away very, very carefully just – sort of – moved, all by themselves. And then she got into trouble. It wasn't fair at all.

BEL MOONEY

I can't find it!

Illustrated by Margaret Chamberlain

MAMMOTH

First published in 1988
by Methuen Children's Books
Published 1989 by Mammoth
an imprint of Mandarin Paperbacks
Michelin House, 81 Fulham Road, London SW3 6RB
Reprinted 1989 (twice)

Mandarin is an imprint of the Octopus Publishing Group

Text copyright © 1988 by Bel Mooney
Illustrations copyright © 1988 by Margaret Chamberlain

ISBN 0 7497 0030 0

A CIP catalogue record for this title
is available from the British Library

Printed in Great Britain
by Cox & Wyman Ltd, Reading

Contents

I can't find my Shoe

Kitty was always losing things. It wasn't that she was careless. Of course not. What happened was this. Things she put away very, very carefully just – sort of – moved, all by themselves. And then she got into trouble. It wasn't fair at all.

One morning Kitty was getting ready for school. She found her vest and pants – under the bed. She found her school dress – in the toy box. She found her cardigan – wrapped round one of her teddies. She found her clean socks in the drawer – which surprised her, because that was were they should be.

One shoe was inside Kitty's bed. She knew it must have hopped there itself, because she remembered putting both shoes neatly by her bed the night before.

Kitty's Mum came into the room. She was looking for her watch. 'Oh, hurry up, Kitty,' she said. 'Why do you always have to be so slow in the morning? Now – where's your other shoe?'

'I can't find it,' Kitty said, in a rather muffled voice, because her head was under the quilt.

'What are you doing in there?' Mum asked her.

'Looking for the shoe, of course,' said Kitty.

'Why would it be in bed, you silly thing?'

'Because that's where the other one walked to,' Kitty said, pulling her head out. She frowned at her mother for not under-standing.

Kitty's Mum looked all round the room, then sighed.

'You'll just have to go to school in your old trainers.'

'But I'll get into trouble,' said Kitty.

'Well, I'm afraid that will teach you not to lose things,' said Mum, gently.

At breakfast Kitty was so quiet that even Dad noticed. Usually she talked to him while he was reading the newspaper, and he said, 'Um' and 'Ah', even though he wasn't really listening. Today it seemed very quiet, so he looked up and asked what was the matter.

'She's lost a shoe,' said Daniel, munching his toast.

'As usual,' said Mum.

'And I've just remembered something else,' said Kitty unhappily.

'What's that?' asked Dad.

'I don't know where my satchel is either.'

Mum groaned. 'Oh no! What am I going to do with you?'

Kitty jumped up and looked all

round the kitchen, even in the fridge – which made Daniel laugh. 'As if your satchel would be in there!'

'Nothing would surprise me,' said Dad.

Mum was thinking hard. 'You can always find things if you remember what you were doing when you last had them,' she said, 'so what did you do when you came home from school last night?'

Kitty thought, and ran out of the room. Suddenly, she knew what had happened.

When she had come home from school she had wanted to watch children's television, but her teacher had given them some spellings to learn. Not easy ones. Hard ones. Kitty thought that if her Mum saw the spelling book inside her satchel she wouldn't let her watch television.

She remembered that one of the words they had to learn was 'Table', so she had hidden the satchel under the table on the landing – which had a long lace cloth on it, right down to the ground.

Kitty ran upstairs, and looked underneath the cloth. Sure enough, there was the satchel. Quickly, she picked it up and peered inside. And tucked down beside her spelling book, was – the missing shoe. But Kitty hadn't the faintest idea how it had got there.

Mum came up the stairs behind her. 'Kitty!' she said in a cross voice. 'What on earth was your satchel doing underneath that table?'

Kitty didn't answer. Instead she just pulled out the shoe, and held it up in the air with a smile. 'Mum,' she said, 'I think I'm really clever. If I hadn't lost my satchel, I wouldn't ever have found my shoe!'

'You always win, Kitty,' said Mum.

I can't find my Teddy

There were lots of teddies on the shelf in Kitty's room, and she liked them all very much indeed. But one of them was special. Very special. He was the oldest of the teddies, and his fur was very worn. Daniel had been given him when he was born, but now he lived with Kitty because Daniel said he was too old for teddy bears. The old bear was small, with a squashy nose, and two pink paws, and sparkling brown glass eyes. Kitty called him Mr Tubs, because of his fat tummy. She liked him best of all because he had a lovely old, warm smell that made her feel at home. He smelt of lots of hugs.

One night, in winter, Kitty was getting ready for bed. At first, she couldn't find her pyjamas, but Mum said she should look under the bed first. And of course they were there.

Kitty washed her face and cleaned her teeth without making too much fuss, then ran into Dan's room to say goodnight. Although Dan was older than Kitty he was already in bed, because he had been off school all day with a bad cold. He looked at her sleepily over the bedclothes.

'Goo-ni,' he mumbled, sniffing.

'Goodnight Daniel,' Kitty said. Secretly she liked it when her brother was a bit sick – not because she was mean, but because he seemed younger, and she could be kind to him. When Kitty was ill, Daniel was nice to her too. Brothers and sisters are like that.

14

Kitty went into her own room, where her Mum was waiting. 'Now, have you got your book, Kitty?' she asked. Kitty looked around – and found the book on the floor under her desk, making a garage for a toy car. Then she jumped into bed at last . . .

'Oh no!' she shouted.

'What's the matter?' Mum asked.

'Where's Mr Tubs? He was in here this morning.'

Mum sighed. 'Kitty – you're *always* losing things,' she said. 'And I thought you loved your teddy too!'

'I do love him,' Kitty almost shouted.

15

'Then why have you lost him?' asked Mum.

Kitty didn't hear. She was burrowing down under the quilt like a little mole. So many things always hid themselves there . . . But at last her head came out of the bottom. 'He isn't in there,' she said.

They looked under the bed. They peered beneath the chest of drawers. They searched the cupboard. They emptied the laundry basket. And they pulled all the other soft toys off their shelf, just in case Mr Tubs was hiding behind them. But there was no sign of the teddy.

Just then, Dad came into the room. 'What's the matter, Kit?' he asked.

'I can't find my teddy,' she wailed.

'Never mind, we'll find him tomorrow,' Dad said.

That made Kitty cross. 'You KNOW I can't sleep without him. You KNOW I can't!' she shouted.

'Well, we'll just have to find him then,' said Mum.

When Mum had walked all over the house, looking for Mr Tubs, and Dad had been out to the garage to see if he was in the car, and Kitty had even pulled everything out of the airing cupboard – they all met again on the landing.

'Oh no,' sighed Mum, looking at the jumble of clean clothes on the floor.

'Oh no,' groaned Dad, looking at his watch and remembering he was missing a good programme on the television.

'Oh nooooo,' cried Kitty, thinking of poor Mr Tubs.

Then Dad had an idea. 'Where would Mr Tubs *want* to be?' he asked.

Kitty thought, 'In bed with me,' she said.

'Yes, but *why*?'

'Because he's kind and he's cuddly, of course.'

'Mmmmm, I wonder . . . ?' said Mum, thoughtfully, looking quickly towards the door of Daniel's room.

Kitty ran in. She could hear her brother breathing like a very puffy train. She tiptoed to the bed, and prodded all the humps and bumps carefully. What was that . . . ? A stubby paw? A fat round tummy? A funny squashy nose?

She slid her hand beneath the bedclothes, and felt about and . . . pulled out Mr Tubs. He was all warm, and he smelt *wonderful*. 'Hallo, Mr Tubs,' she whispered. 'Did my horrid old brother steal you away?'

Mum and Dad had followed her into the room. They smiled down at Daniel, and at Kitty and the teddy.

'Daniel didn't steal him,' whispered Mum, 'I think he just wanted some comfort – don't you?'

'Because when you're ill, you want something to hug – even if you're big,' said Dad.

Kitty nodded. She looked from Mr Tubs to Daniel and back again. Mr Tubs looked very happy. 'What will Dan think if he wakes up and finds him gone?' she asked, slowly.

18

'He'll be sad and think, "I can't find my teddy", and *you* know how sad that is,' said Mum.

'Well, do you think I should leave Mr Tubs with Daniel, just for tonight?' said Kitty, feeling very grown-up.

'Yes, I think you should,' said Mum, smiling at Kitty.

And so she did.

I can't find
my Pretty Clothes

It was Saturday – Kitty's favourite day. She was looking forward to playing in her room, and making a mess, and running in the garden, and . . . 'Now Kitty,' said Mum, 'It's Melissa's birthday party today. Had you forgotten?'

Kitty groaned out loud. Then she banged her mug on the table. Then she kicked the table leg. Then she folded her arms crossly and frowned.

Daniel laughed, as usual. 'Oh Kitty-witty, must look pretty,' he sang, ducking as she threw a crust across the table at his head.

Mum clapped her hands. 'That's quite enough,' she said sternly. 'It'll be very nice for you to go to your cousin's party.'

'At least I'll get a going-home bag,' said Kitty gloomily.

She remembered the last time Melissa had a party. Two hours before they had to leave Mum had put her in the bath, to scrub her clean – which took quite a long time. She had washed Kitty's hair and tied it back with two blue *ribbons*. Ribbons! In Kitty's hair! Then she had made Kitty put on the brand new pretty dress she had bought specially. It was pale blue with lots of little white flowers all over it, and a white lace collar and cuffs. Clean white shoes and socks finished Kitty's party clothes.

It was terrible.

Mum had put her in front of the mirror. 'There,' she said. 'Don't you look pretty?'

'I look yukky,' growled Kitty, staring at herself.

'Quite right!' laughed Daniel. '*Pretty-pretty* Kitty-witty.'

'OH SHUT UP!' she had shouted.

That was a year ago. So now Kitty thought for a moment and said, 'My dress won't fit me now.'

'Yes, it will,' said Mum. 'I got it out, and measured it. It was a little bit big last year, so this year it's perfect.'

'Oh,' said Kitty, sticking out her lip in a sulk. There was nothing she could do.

Or – was there?

The day passed quickly, and it was soon time. After the bath, Mum folded Kitty in a big warm towel and said, 'Now run into your room and bring your pretty clothes in here. The hair ribbons are on the hanger too . . .'

Kitty went into her room. Then, after a while, she called, 'I can't find my pretty clothes,' trying to sound worried.

Mum came out of the bathroom. 'But I know they were in your wardrobe. I saw them the other day!'

'I didn't,' said Kitty.

Mum looked on the rail, then pulled open

Kitty's drawers. She frowned at the mess. 'Now, where *can* that party dress be?' she said.

'Oh Mum, I don't know,' said Kitty. 'You know I'm always losing things.' She crossed her fingers behind her back, and looked up at the ceiling.

Just then Dad came into the room. 'What's all the fuss about?' he asked.

Mum looked flustered. She explained, and shook her head. 'That's the only pretty dress she's got. I'll have to ring up Susan and say she can't come to the party.'

Dad looked at Kitty. She stopped the smile that had started to turn up the corners of her mouth, and put a sad look on her face.

'Oh, I don't know,' he said slowly, still staring at her. 'I think she should go anyway – in the clothes she was wearing earlier.'

Mum looked at Kitty, and Kitty looked at her dirty clothes. Her jumper was covered in clay, and she had wiped her hands on her jeans, and her old trainers were brown with dried mud. It was how she liked to look. But for Melissa's party . . .

'Right! In the car now!' said Dad.

Of course, Kitty's cousin Melissa *always* looked pretty, and for her own birthday party she was wearing a dress that looked like a snowflake. Six other little girls gathered behind her at the door, all wearing their best party clothes. They giggled when they saw Kitty. She felt awful.

'My cousin's really *scruffy*,' said Melissa with her nose in the air.

Kitty felt even worse.

After the games, and the tea, and more games, it was time for Dad to come and collect her. Kitty said nothing all the way

home. She didn't even look into her going-home bag to see what was there.

As soon as they reached home, Kitty went upstairs. She crept into the spare room, and opened the door of the bedside cupboard. There, crumpled in a bundle, were her party dress, the blue ribbons, the white socks and the shoes. She took them all back into her own room, and put them in her wardrobe.

She had just finished when Dad came in. 'Do you think you'll ever find your party clothes, Kit?' he asked.

'I expect so,' she mumbled, trying not to look guilty.

'Well,' said Dad, looking wise, 'maybe you couldn't find them today – but you found something else instead, didn't you?'

26

'What?' Kitty asked.

'You found it's not very nice to look scruffy when people expect you not to – is it?'

'No, Dad,' said Kitty.

'And maybe you'll find you won't tell fibs in the future. Am I right?'

'Yes, Dad,' Kitty said.

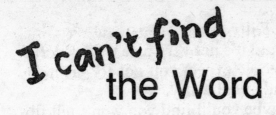 I can't find the Word

It really was not fair, Kitty thought one day, how when you were really cross with some-one, and wanted to tell them – all the words disappeared out of your head. That is – all the *good* words. Easy words came rushing into your mind, but they just made you sound babyish. Hard words, really grown-up words, were much harder to find. But they were the ones that would say what you *really* felt. So, when Daniel borrowed her new pen-cil and lost it, she lost her temper. 'Oh you . . . you . . . you . . . fat pig!' she shouted.

Mum frowned at her over the newspaper. 'Honestly, Kitty. If you're going to be rude to your brother you might as well be rude in an intelligent way.'

'Er . . . what do you mean?' Kitty asked.

'I mean that you might as well call him something that makes sense. Like a . . . a . . . careless robber, or something.'

'I'm not a robber!' yelled Daniel.

'Well, you stole my pencil, didn't you – you . . . you . . . you . . . oooh, I don't know what to call you,' shouted Kitty, running out of the room.

But before she closed the door she heard her brother say, 'Poor Kitty can't find the right word.' He sounded very pleased with himself.

Where do you *find* words? Kitty wondered, lying on her bed. She thought that there might be a sort of box in your mind, a treasure chest full of words, just waiting for you to open it up, and take them out one by one. Then, after a while, you would never have to search for a word. The right one would just jump out of the box, ready to do as you wished. And once that happened, *nobody* would be able to get the better of you, Kitty decided. Not at all. But where do the words come from?

Dad was in his bedroom, listening to the radio. People were talking about politics. There were plenty of words there – all flying out into the air.

Then Kitty wandered downstairs to the sitting room, where there was an enormous bookcase, crammed with books. Plenty of words there too – all locked between the pages. At last she went back into the kitchen, where her mother still sat at the kitchen table, reading the newspaper. That was packed with words too – all dancing about on the large white pages.

Daniel had gone into the garden. So Kitty pulled at Mum's sleeve, and asked, 'Mum – how do *you* find the word you want?'

Mum laughed. 'Sometimes it's hard for grown-ups too,' she said, 'but I know what I do. I read and read and read, and that way I keep putting words into my brain, ready for

when I need them. Like saving up pocket money. A long time – *hundreds* of years ago – they used to call that your own Word-hoard.'

Kitty was excited. 'That's just the way I pictured it!' she said.

'The other thing,' said Mum, 'is not to get cross. When you lose your temper you lose your words as well. People huff and puff, like you do. *That's* no good at all.'

Kitty shook her head. Then Mum got up from the table, and held out her hand to Kitty. 'Come with me,' she said.

They went upstairs again to Daniel's room. Mum searched in his untidy book-

31

case, until she pulled out a large red book.
'What does that say?' she asked Kitty.

Kitty frowned, and after a little while she
said slowly, 'Jun-ior Dic-shun-erry.'

'That's right,' Mum said. 'Now if you curl
up in a corner with this, you'll find you meet
lots of new words, and some of them might
be very useful!'

Kitty found it hard at first, but soon she
forgot everything. It was such fun to dip into
the book, and read the words (sometimes

that took a little time), and find out what they meant. It was like a new game, and she loved it.

That evening the family sat down together to have supper. Kitty was in a bad mood again, because Daniel had wanted to watch his programme on the television, and Kitty had wanted another one. They quarrelled in the sitting room, and they kicked each other under the table, then Mum burnt her finger on the cooker and she got cross too.

'I haven't got any gravy,' Kitty said in a bossy voice.

'Here – I'll pour some for you,' said Mum.

'I didn't want it *there*, I wanted it *there*, on the potatoes,' Kitty said crossly.

Mum put the jug down, and looked at her. 'Now just stop being so . . . so . . . oh, I don't know the word for what you're being!'

'Aggressive,' Kitty said, pleased. She folded her arms and grinned at her mother. 'You're losing all *your* words now, Mum!'

I can't find my Courage

Kitty was brave. She never *ever* cried. Or at least, that was what she told her friends at school. Of course, we all cry when we are hurt – even Kitty. And one Saturday, at the swimming pool, she cried a lot.

This is how it happened. Kitty was a good swimmer, and loved to dive into the water. Her Dad always said she was like a little fish. He also told her never to play in a silly way at the swimming pool, because you can get hurt. 'Look at those boys,' he said. 'That's what I mean.'

Some older boys were jumping into the water in a way that made a big splash. They called it 'dive bombs'. It made other people rush to get out of the way. The boys laughed a lot, but Kitty's Dad frowned. 'They're just stupid,' he said.

But Kitty thought it looked fun. She watched for a while. Then she stood on the edge of the pool. Dad and Daniel were in the water. 'Why shouldn't I?' thought Kitty.

SPLASH!

'Owwwwwwwwwwwww!'

It was a horrible feeling. Kitty felt as if the water had jumped up to slap her hard on her arms and legs. When she did her proper dives she slid *through* the water. This time she fell *at* the water – and it hurt.

'Ow-oww-owww-owwww!'

She cried and cried, and Dad cuddled her. He didn't say 'I told you not to do that', or 'Silly girl', or anything like that. He just whispered, 'Poor Kitty-Kat, does it tingle?' and held her close.

'Can we go home now, Daddy?' she asked in a little snuffly voice. Usually she had to be *made* to get out of the water, but Kitty had had enough swimming for one day!

Four days later was the day Kitty went swimming with her class at school. She usually looked forward to it. To be honest, that was because she was one of the best swimmers in the class, and liked showing off – just a little bit.

'Right children, today we're going to do some dives,' said Miss Evans. 'Hands up those who can already dive!'

Kitty put her hand up.

'All right then, Kitty, you can show us,' said Miss Evans with a smile.

Kitty stepped to the edge of the pool. She looked down. The water blinked and flashed at her. It looked fierce. It looked as though it might hit her again, and make her arms and legs tingle.

'Come on, Kitty!' called her friends.

She waited, with her arms stretched out. But she could not dive in.

Miss Evans was jolly and kind, and could see that something was wrong. So quickly she told the class to get into the water and practise their swimming. Then she came up to Kitty. 'What's the matter, Kitty?' she asked.

'I . . . I . . .' Kitty stammered.

'Yes?'

'I can't . . . find my . . . courage,' said Kitty in a small voice.

She told Miss Evans what had happened on Saturday. Miss Evans nodded. 'What we say is, you've lost your nerve,' she said, 'so now you must find it again, Kitty.'

'But *where* do I look for it?' asked Kitty.

'Where you last had it, of course!' said Miss Evans. 'Listen, when you fall off a horse, or a bike, it's very important to get back on again – right away. On Saturday you should have done a proper dive as soon as you stopped hurting. That way you find your courage exactly where you lost it.'

'Oh,' said Kitty. 'So I have to look for it in *there*.' And she pointed to the water.

'Yes,' said Miss Evans, taking her hand and standing on the edge of the pool. 'And I'm going to help you look. Shall we dive in together?'

'I'm afraid the water will hit me again,' Kitty said.

Miss Evans shook her head. 'It won't hurt you if you're kind to it! If *you* don't hit *it*! You see? Trust me.'

Kitty nodded.

'Get ready,' said Miss Evans, 'and go when I count to three.'

Kitty took a deep breath. She stretched out her arms, and bent her knees, and waited.

'One . . . two . . . THREE!'

It was a lovely feeling. The cool water rushed past her ears – and in a second she was up again. Miss Evans' head bobbed next to hers. She smiled. 'And how did that feel, Kitty?' she asked.

Instead of answering, Kitty ducked her head forward and did something Daniel had taught her on Saturday, before her awful jump. It was a handstand under water.

She came up shaking the water out of her eyes, and laughing.

'And what were you doing down there?' Miss Evans smiled.

'I was finding some *more* courage at the bottom of the pool,' Kitty panted, 'so now I'll never lose it again!'

I can't find my Way

It was a lovely summer Sunday, and Kitty woke up early. The birds were singing in the garden. The sun shone through the curtains on Mr Tub's twinkling glass eyes. She could hear Mum and Dad moving around downstairs already.

Kitty felt excited. They were going on a picnic today. There was a beautiful old house, a really big one, in the countryside near them, and you could pay to visit it. 'We'll have a look at all the lovely things in the house, and then have a picnic in the gardens,' said Mum.

'There's a maze too,' said Dad.

'Oh good. And can we have salad sandwiches?' asked Daniel.

'Do we have to look at the things in the house?' asked Kitty, grumpily.

But that was the night before. Now she felt in a good mood, and jumped up to dress. It was funny, but when she did not have to go to school she could always find her

clothes. So, soon she was having her breakfast – and then it was time to go.

When they reached Barrington Manor,
Kitty gasped. The old house was black and
white with tall chimneys, and little windows
with diamond panes of glass. The gardens
were full of bushes and trees, and places to
hide – and all Kitty wanted to do was play.
But when they parked in the car park, Mum
said to Dad, 'I can't wait to see all that
wonderful old furniture,' and Dad said, 'I
hear there are fine suits of armour.' And
Kitty felt bored at the thought of the house.

'I don't want to look at silly old furniture,' she said, stamping her foot.

'Come on, Kitty-Kat,' said Dad, taking hold of her hand, 'it'll be really interesting, you see.'

As they walked along the path to the house, Kitty saw a sign saying, 'To the maze'. She pulled her father's hand. 'Let's just go and look at it, just for a minute,' she pleaded, and he agreed.

When they reached the maze, all Kitty could see were hedges. It didn't look very exciting, or very difficult. Mum said, 'Come *on*! I want to look at the house', and then Kitty did a very naughty thing indeed. She pulled her hand out of Dad's, and ran into the maze. 'Can't catch me', she called over her shoulder.

She ran down a little path, with a wall of hedge each side, and turned a corner, then another corner. She could hear Daniel calling, 'Kitty – come back!' and Mum telling her not to be so naughty.

'I'll just hide for a few minutes and then go back,' Kitty thought, skipping a bit further along the path, then turning another way, and then another. 'Come and find me!' she shouted, but her voice sounded small – muffled by the high hedges. 'You can't find me!' she shouted again – but a bird sang

loudly somewhere near her, and she suddenly couldn't hear her parents at all.

'I think I'll go back now,' Kitty said to herself, turning back the way she had come. But there were two ways to go – which was the right one? She chose one path, but then it turned off sharply towards the middle of the maze. Or was that the way out? She didn't know. It all looked the same.

Kitty remembered Hansel and Gretel in the wood, and wished she had dropped something so that she could find her way out. Or left Dad holding a long thread . . . But it was no good thinking that. She must be brave, and find the right path somehow.

'Daddy!' she called, and thought she heard his voice say 'Hallo'. But it seemed a long way away. Kitty started to walk more quickly. Then she began to run, on and on, further and further, round and round – until she felt quite dizzy. And she felt tears come into her eyes.

At last, turning a corner, she went *crash* – into someone coming towards her. It was a young woman wearing jeans, with long dark hair and a headband round it. She had a kind, suntanned face, and was carrying a pair of garden shears. 'Hallo,' she said, looking at Kitty's face. 'What's the matter?'

Kitty sniffed, 'I . . . can't . . . find . . .

my . . . way.'

The girl smiled, 'Well, you're lucky. I'm Sally, one of the gardeners, and I know the way out. Come on.' And she took Kitty's hand, turned her round, and started slowly to take her out of the maze.

As they walked she told Kitty wonderful stories about Barrington Manor, and how there was a friendly lady ghost who lived in the blue bedroom, and how if you shouted in one corridor you would hear two echoes, and how the maze was built in the days when ladies wore huge white ruffs right up to their ears, and you could see dresses like that in the house . . .

At last they reached the entrance, where Mum and Dad and Daniel were standing, looking a bit worried. 'Oh, *there* you are,' called Mum. 'Dad was just going to find someone to help us.'

'Well, *I* found someone,' said Kitty happily, looking up at Sally. 'I couldn't find my way, and I got a bit scared, but then I found Sally, and she's a gardener, and she works here, and she's been telling me all sorts of things, and can we go and see the house now, Mum?'

Mum laughed. 'Phew,' she said. 'Kitty, I'm a-*mazed*!'

I can't find my List

Kitty's Mum stood in the kitchen and folded her arms. 'If you say "I can't find it" one more time,' she said, 'I'll *scream*.'

Kitty wasn't listening. She was rummaging in the toy box, throwing things all over the floor. At last she sat back and said, 'I can't find one of my roller skates.'

Daniel grinned. 'Go on then Mum,' he said, 'SCREAM.'

And she did.

'Whatever's going on?' asked Dad, coming into the room.

Mum said nothing, so Daniel explained. 'Well, first of all Kitty lost her toothbrush. Then she couldn't find her sandals. Then she lost her pocket money, which Mum had only just given to her. Then she started to eat a biscuit and put it down somewhere and couldn't find the bit that was left. Then she lost Mum's purse, when Mum asked her to fetch it so she could give her more pocket money. And then she couldn't find . . .'

Kitty scowled. 'Tell-tale,' she said.

'No, he's not,' said Dad. 'I asked, and he told me, that's all. He's not trying to get you into trouble, are you, Dan?'

Daniel hid his grin. 'No,' he said, looking very good.

They all looked at Kitty, and she looked back at them. Then her mouth turned down at the corners. It wasn't fair, she thought. Everybody was against her. And it wasn't her fault that she lost things. It was so exciting to rush from one game to another, and there was so much to think about, you couldn't remember things. It wasn't her fault.

'Why doesn't Daniel forget things and lose things?' she asked, quietly.

'Because I'm clever,' he said, in an important voice.

Kitty's mouth turned down even more, and Mum felt sorry for her. 'It's got nothing to do with being clever,' she said. And she took Kitty on her knee, whilst Dad started to make a salad for lunch. 'Let's talk about it, Kit,' she said, 'and see what we can do about it. Now – *why* do you lose things?'

'Because I forget where they are,' said Kitty, 'I forget to remember where I put them.'

'Is it because your room's a mess?' asked Mum, gently.

'Yes,' said Kitty.

'Well, I know what the answer is,' said Dad, shaking lettuce leaves in the sink. 'Organisation!'

'What?' Kitty asked.

'Or-gan-is-a-tion,' he said again. 'It means a tidy mind. It means a tidy room. It means making lists.'

'What sort of lists?' asked Kitty.

'Well, you should have a list of all the things you need to take to school, and then you wouldn't lose them.'

To be truthful, Kitty couldn't quite see why this would work. But she liked the idea. It sounded fun. 'I'll get a notebook and pencil,' she said, rushing to the sideboard. But after a few moments she came back. 'I can't

50

find a pencil,' she said.

'Right, that's it,' said Mum. 'We'll start by having your room tidied today – so that you know that pencils are in one drawer in your desk, notebooks in another, and plasticine in another. It will make life much easier. And you can make a list of all the things, and a list of everything you need to take to school, so that each night you can get them all ready. And then you won't lose things.'

'It's a brilliant idea,' said Dad.

All afternoon Kitty worked. Mum came to help her. The clothes were put in the right drawers in little piles, all Kitty's toys were sorted out on different shelves in her cupboard, and all her art stuff was arranged in the different places in her little desk. Even the teddies were put tidily on their shelf, although Mr Tubs didn't look as if he liked it.

As she did it, Kitty made a little list in her notebook. It said things like, 'Monday. Art

Club. Apron in Bottom Drawer', and so on. Except that sometimes she spelt the words wrongly.

At last it was all finished. Kitty was proud of her list, and showed everyone. Then she went out into the garden to play for a while. She swung on the swing, and she rode her bicycle, and she chased butterflies. Then Daniel suggested they play a game of hide and seek all over the house until it was time for bed.

'Oh, I wish it wasn't school tomorrow,' said Kitty, when she had had her bath.

'Nonsense,' said Mum, 'because now you're like a new girl. Now you're an organised girl, aren't you?'

Kitty nodded. It was true. Everything was going to be different now. 'Good girl,' said Mum. 'Now you go into your bedroom, and get all your things ready for me to see. And in the morning we'll have a nice peaceful time instead of the usual rush.'

Kitty went into her room. It looked horrid, she thought, all neat – like a room nobody lived in. Now . . . time to get everything ready . . .

Oh dear. She looked in the pocket of the dirty jeans she had been wearing, and then in her jacket in the wardrobe, and then underneath the teddies, and then in her desk drawers, and then amongst her clothes. But it was nowhere to be found.

After a while Kitty's Mum and Dad came into the room. 'Now look,' her mother was saying, 'she's been such a good . . . OH NO!'

The room looked as if a whirlwind had swept it up into the air and then dropped it again. Kitty was kneeling and rummaging in the bottom of her wardrobe. She stuck her head out cheerfully, and said, 'Guess what? I can't find my list. That must make it a lost list!'

'Oh, *Kitty*!' was all they could say.

I can't find
the Car Keys

It was Saturday morning in Kitty's house. Mum was taking Dad to the dentist, then taking Kitty and Daniel shopping, and then they were going to the swimming baths. Kitty didn't like the shopping much, but she wanted to go swimming, and so she said nothing. Anyway, Mum had said she might buy her a new drawing book.

For once she was ready on time. She had her anorak on, and her swimming costume wrapped in her towel under her arm – and waited by the front door. Daniel came down next. He looked surprised to see Kitty there before him, and stood with her.

'Where's Mum?' asked Kitty.

'Getting ready,' said Dan. 'You know how long she takes!'

Dad came out of the sitting room and stood with them. After a while he looked at his watch and shouted up the stairs. 'Hurry up, love! The children are all ready!'

After a while Kitty's Mum came running

down the stairs looking worried. She went
into the kitchen, and came out. She went into
the sitting room, and came out. Then she
went upstairs again.

'What are you looking for?' asked Dad.

'I can't find the car keys,' she called.

Dad groaned. 'Oh no,' he said, 'I'll be late for my appointment.'

Kitty's Mum came down again, and

emptied her handbag on the hall table. Kitty stared. It was such a messy pile of papers and tissues and bottles of scent and make-up and bus tickets and pens and pencils and half-finished rolls of sweets . . . . 'Yuk,' said Kitty.

'Messy Mum,' grinned Daniel.

'That's not helpful,' she said crossly.

Dad searched behind all the cushions in the sitting room, and looked on the mantle-piece. Daniel walked up and down the garden path to see if she might have dropped them. Mum ran all over the house, getting more and more bad-tempered. 'Oh, where can they be?' she said.

Now Dad was a bit cross too. 'Can't you remember where you had them last?' he asked.

'In the car! I must have left them in the car!' she said, looking cheerful.

But Dad came in from the garage with empty hands. 'Not there – I do wish you wouldn't lose things,' he said.

'I *don't* lose things – I've only lost the car keys,' said Mum, sounding crosser than ever.

'You always tell me off for losing things, Mum,' Kitty piped up.

'And that's NOT helpful either,' said Mum.

'Better keep out of the way, Kit,' said Daniel, going upstairs to his room.

But Kitty thought and thought. She *was* always getting into trouble for losing things, but that had taught her something. She was sure she could find the car keys, and then Mum and Dad would stop being cross, and then the day would be saved. She *hated* it when her Mum and Dad were angry with each other. She would do anything to stop it.

So she thought even harder. Now . . . when did Mum last use the car?

Yesterday.

But *when* yesterday?

When she had to take that pile of jumble down to the church hall, ready for the sale.

So – what was she wearing?

The answer shone in Kitty's mind like a ray of sunlight.

Kitty's Mum usually wore a comfortable old blue jacket that hung by the kitchen door. She had already looked in its pockets for the car keys.

But Kitty remembered her Mum saying she would probably meet Mrs Briggs at the hall, who was in charge of the jumble sale. Mrs Briggs talked in a funny voice and was rather rich, and bossy, and always wore a coat with a fur collar. Kitty didn't like her much because she always patted her and said, 'And how are we today?', as if she was about two.

For some reason, Mrs Briggs made Kitty's Mum feel nervous. So if she knew she was going to meet her, she wouldn't want to look scruffy . . .

Quickly Kitty ran upstairs. She went into her parents' bedroom, and pulled open the wardrobe door. There was Mum's new purple coat on its hanger, looking funny with its padded shoulders. Kitty put her hand in one pocket. Nothing there. Then in the other pocket . . . and of course there was a jingling sound.

When she came downstairs Dad was standing by the phone. 'It's no good,' he was saying, 'I'll just have to ring up and tell the dentist I'm not coming.'

'Oh, I'm sorry, dear,' said Kitty's Mum, unhappily.

'No, you won't!' called Kitty, coming down the stairs like someone in a play and holding the car keys above her head. 'Just look what *I've* found!'

Dad picked her up and swung her about, just as he used to do when she was very small. Then, when she was on the ground again, Mum knelt down to give her a hug.

'Kitty, you're such a clever girl. How did you know where to look?'

Kitty explained. 'You always tell me to remember what I was doing when I last had the things I lost, don't you, Mum?' she said.

Mum nodded. 'But I still don't know how you thought of looking in my best coat,' she said slowly.

Dad winked at Kitty. 'That's easy,' he said. 'Your daughter *knows* you. She knows you're a bit afraid of posh people, and a bit proud yourself. I'll tell you what. Kitty's found more than the car keys. She's found you out!'

A Selected List of Titles Available from Mammoth

While every effort is made to keep prices low, it is sometimes necessary to increase prices at short notice. Mammoth Paperbacks reserve the right to show new retail prices on covers which may differ from those previously advertised in the text or elsewhere.

The prices shown below were correct at the time of going to press.

☐	416 96490 7	**Dilly the Dinosaur**	Tony Bradman	£1.99
☐	416 51910 5	**The Witch's Big Toe**	Ralph Wright	£1.75
☐	416 95910 5	**The Grannie Season**	Joan Phipson	£1.75
☐	416 58270 2	**Listen to this Story**	Grace Hallworth	£1.75
☐	416 10382 0	**The Knights of Hawthorn Crescent**	Jenny Koralek	£1.50
☐	416 13822 5	**It's Abigail Again**	Moira Miller	£1.99
☐	416 11972 7	**Lucy Jane at the Ballet**	Susan Hampshire	£1.50
☐	416 06432 9	**Alf Gorilla**	Michael Grater	£1.75
☐	416 10362 6	**Owl and Billy**	Martin Waddell	£1.50
☐	416 13122 0	**Hetty Pegler, Half-Witch**	Margaret Greaves	£1.75
☐	416 57290 1	**Flat Stanley**	Jeff Brown	£1.99
☐	416 00572 1	**Princess Polly to the Rescue**	Mary Lister	£1.50
☐	416 00552 7	**Non Stop Nonsense**	Margaret Mahy	£1.75
☐	416 10322 7	**Claudius Bald Eagle**	Sam McBratney	£1.75
☐	416 03212 5	**I Don't Want To!**	Bel Mooney	£1.99

All these books are available at your bookshop or newsagent, or can be ordered direct from the publisher. Just tick the titles you want and fill in the form below.

Mammoth Paperbacks, Cash Sales Department, PO Box 11, Falmouth, Cornwall TR10 9EN.

Please send cheque or postal order, no currency, for purchase price quoted and allow the following for postage and packing:

UK	55p for the first book, 22p for the second book and 14p for each additional book ordered to a maximum charge of £1.75.
BFPO and Eire ·	55p for the first book, 22p for the second book and 14p for each of the next seven books, thereafter 8p per book.
Overseas Customers	£1.00 for the first book plus 25p per copy for each additional book.

NAME (Block Letters) ....

ADDRESS ....

....